BILLIONS
OF
BRICKS

For my parents—thanks for all the bricks —K. C.

Henry Holt and Company, LLC
Publishers since 1866
175 Fifth Avenue
New York, New York 10010
mackids.com

Our books may be purchased in bulk for promotional,
educational, or business use. Please contact your local
bookseller or the Macmillan Corporate and Premium Sales
Department at (800) 221-7945 ext. 5442 or by e-mail
at MacmillanSpecialMarkets@macmillan.com.

Library of Congress Cataloging-in-Publication Data
Names: Cyrus, Kurt, author.
Title: Billions of bricks / Kurt Cyrus.
Description: First edition. | New York : Henry Holt and Company, 2016. |
    Summary: A counting book that leads readers through the
    day in the life of a construction worker building with bricks.
Identifiers: LCCN 2015030945 | ISBN 9781627792738 (hardback)
Subjects: | CYAC: Stories in rhyme. | Building–Fiction. | Bricks–Fiction. |
    Construction workers–Fiction. | Counting. | BISAC: JUVENILE FICTION /
    Concepts / Counting & Numbers.
Classification: LCC PZ8.3.C997 Bil 2016 | DDC [E]–dc23
LC record available at http://lccn.loc.gov/2015030945

First Edition–2016 / Designed by April Ward

Printed in China by RR Donnelley Asia Printing Solutions Ltd.,
Dongguan City, Guangdong Province

10 9 8 7 6 5 4 3 2 1

Kurt Cyrus

Christy Ottaviano Books

Henry Holt and Company

NEW YORK

Two,
   four,
      six.
Look at all the bricks!
Red and rough, hard and tough.
   Two,
      four,
         six.

Ten, twenty, thirty.
Some are old and dirty.
Some are clean or in-between.
Ten, twenty, thirty.

Dig the clay.
Squish it thick.
Take a **mold** and make a **brick**.

Dump it out.
Let it dry.
Stoke the **oven** way up **high**.

Mix, mix, mix
the mortar for the bricks.

Make it sloppy!
Goopy!
Gloppy!
Mix,
mix,
mix.

Bricks and blocks abound.
Build beneath the ground!
Arches, pillars,
walls, and cellars,
winding all around.

Five, ten,
fifteen, twenty.
Stacks of bricks,
bricks aplenty!

Lay them at your feet.
Fit them nice and neat.
Four by four, then more and more—
repeat. Repeat. Repeat!

On it goes, in rows and rows,
and soon you have a **street**.

Two,
 four,
  six.
Another batch of bricks!
Big and small, we use them all.
Two, four, six.

Build a solid base.
Lock them into place.

Ten,
twenty,
thirty,
forty,
filling every space.

Clack! Clack! Clack!
Bricks can break your back.
Bend your knees when lifting, please.
Clack! Clack! Clack!

Stack them to the sky,
a hundred meters high.
Twenty,
forty,
sixty,
eighty,
straight into the sky.

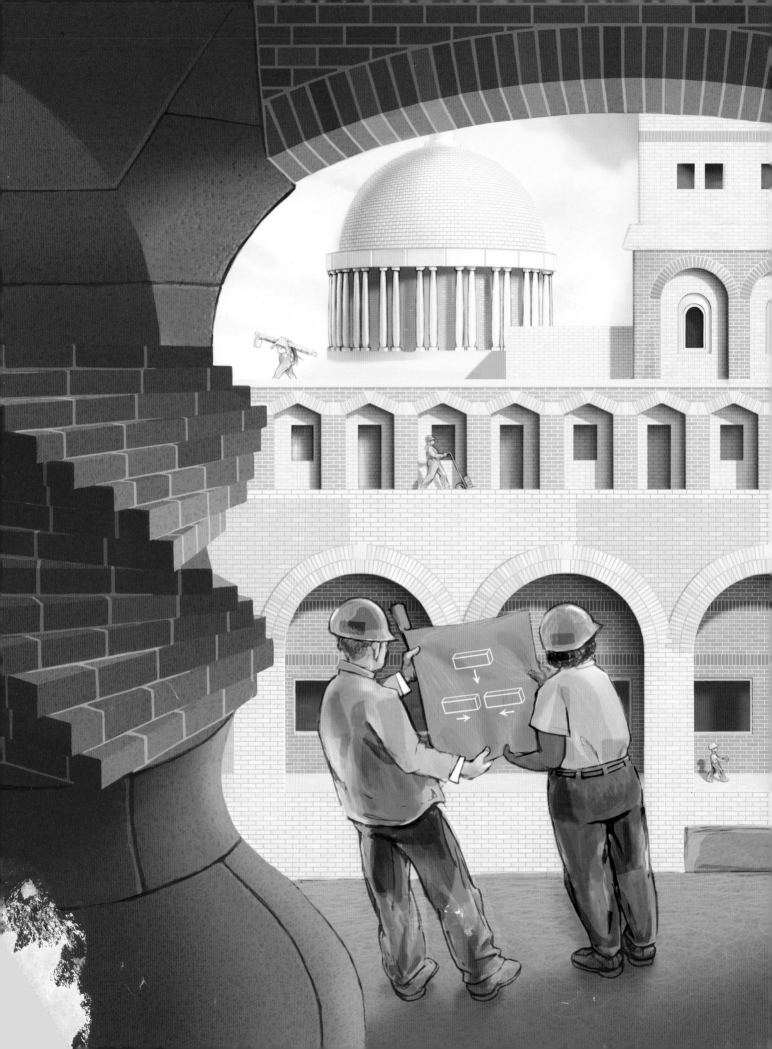

Two,
four,
six.
A million, billion bricks.
Columns, walls, shopping malls,
halls of politics.

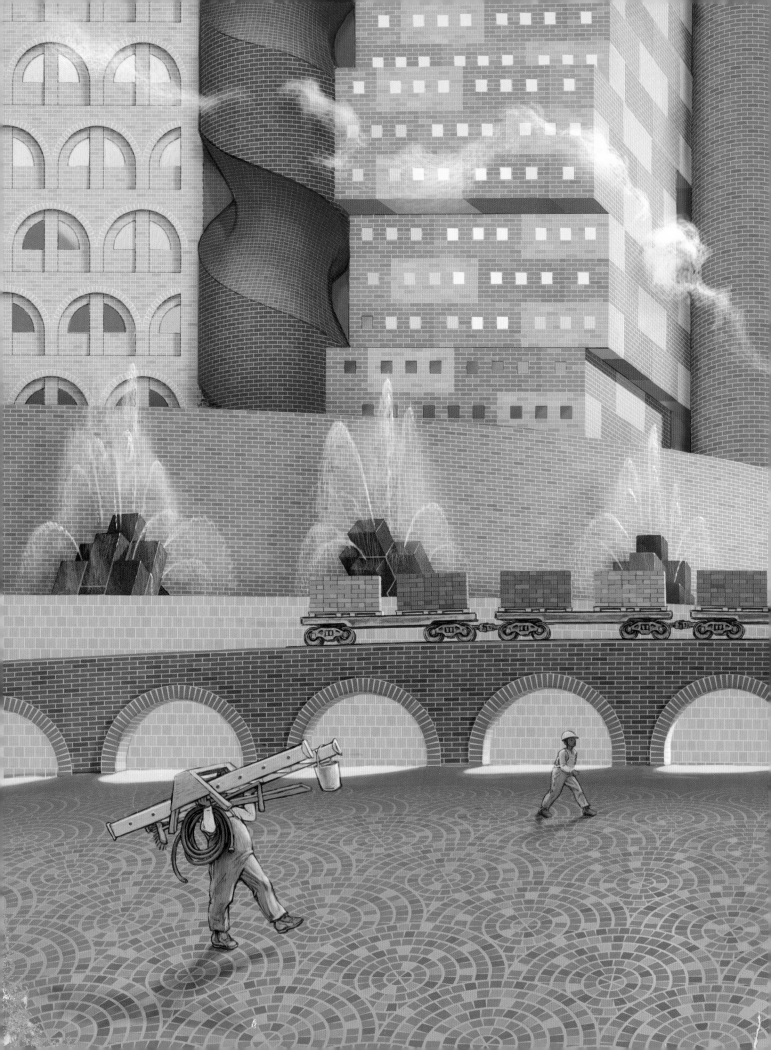

Grand hotels.
Wishing wells.
Railroad yards.
Boulevards.
Fountains! Pools!
Public schools!

This whole book is full of bricks,
and now that it's been written,
we couldn't stack another block
for all the **bricks** in **Britain**.

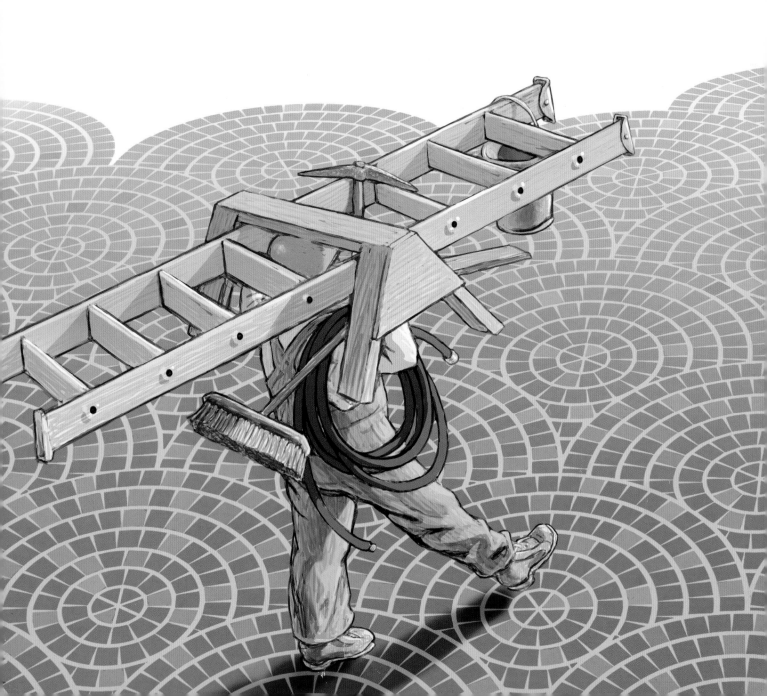

The work is nearly done.
The cleanup has begun.
Let's count the bricks we didn't use...
All together—

one.